BIG ★ KID POWER

I Use the POTTY

Maria van Lieshout

chronicle books · san francisco

When I was a baby, I drank lots of milk.

GLUG

GLUG

GLUG

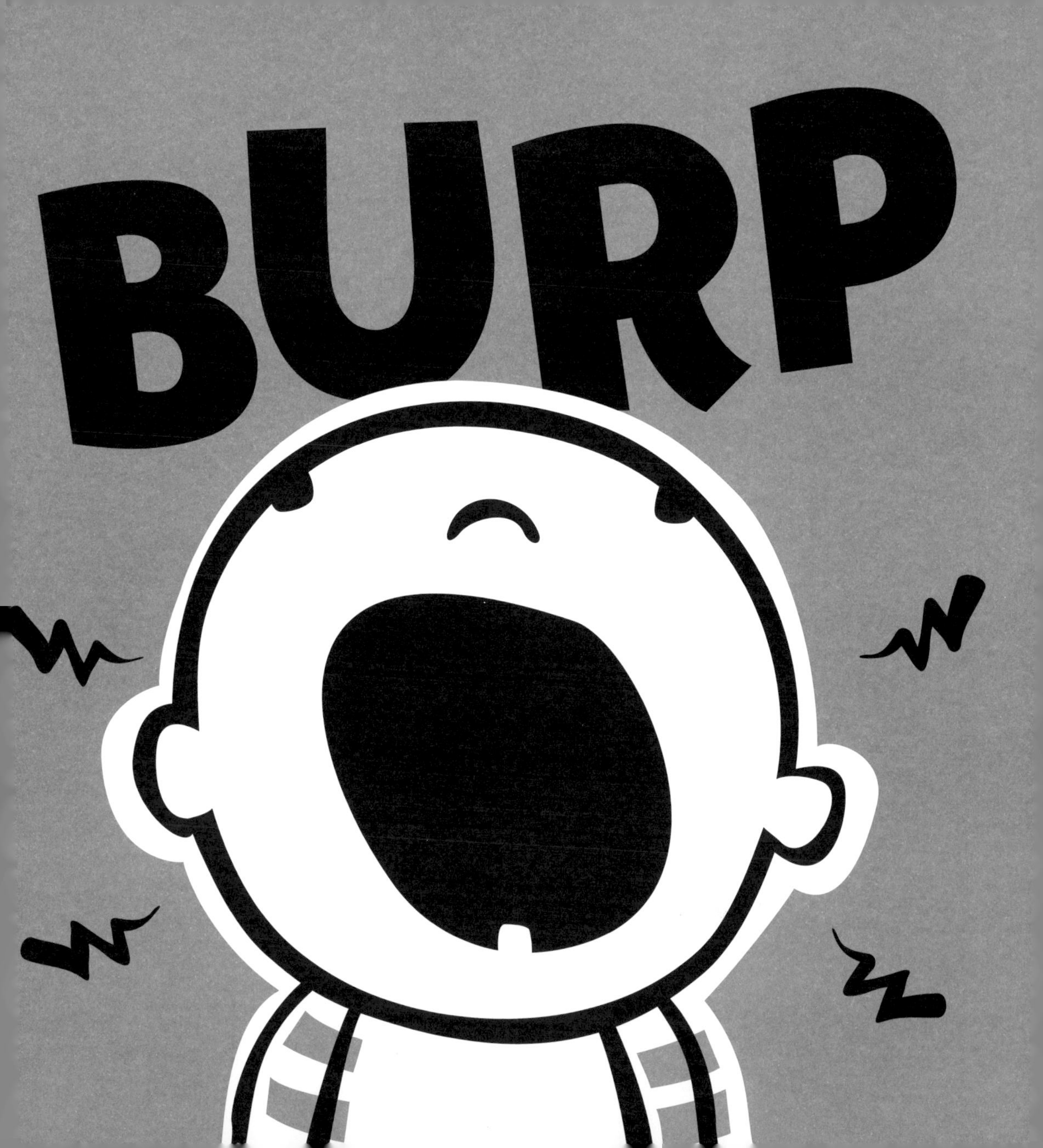
BURP

And I peed and pooped...

ALL.
THE.
TIME.

I pooped and peed in

SO
MANY
DIAPERS.

YUCKY, STINKY DIAPERS!

Do I still pee and poop in a diaper?

NO,
BIG KIDS
USE THE
POTTY.

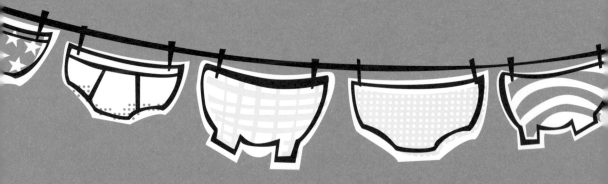

Big kids wear

UNDERW

When I have
to go . . .

I go into the bathroom,
pull down my undies,
and sit on the potty.

Sometimes it takes a while.

But then . . .

PLOP

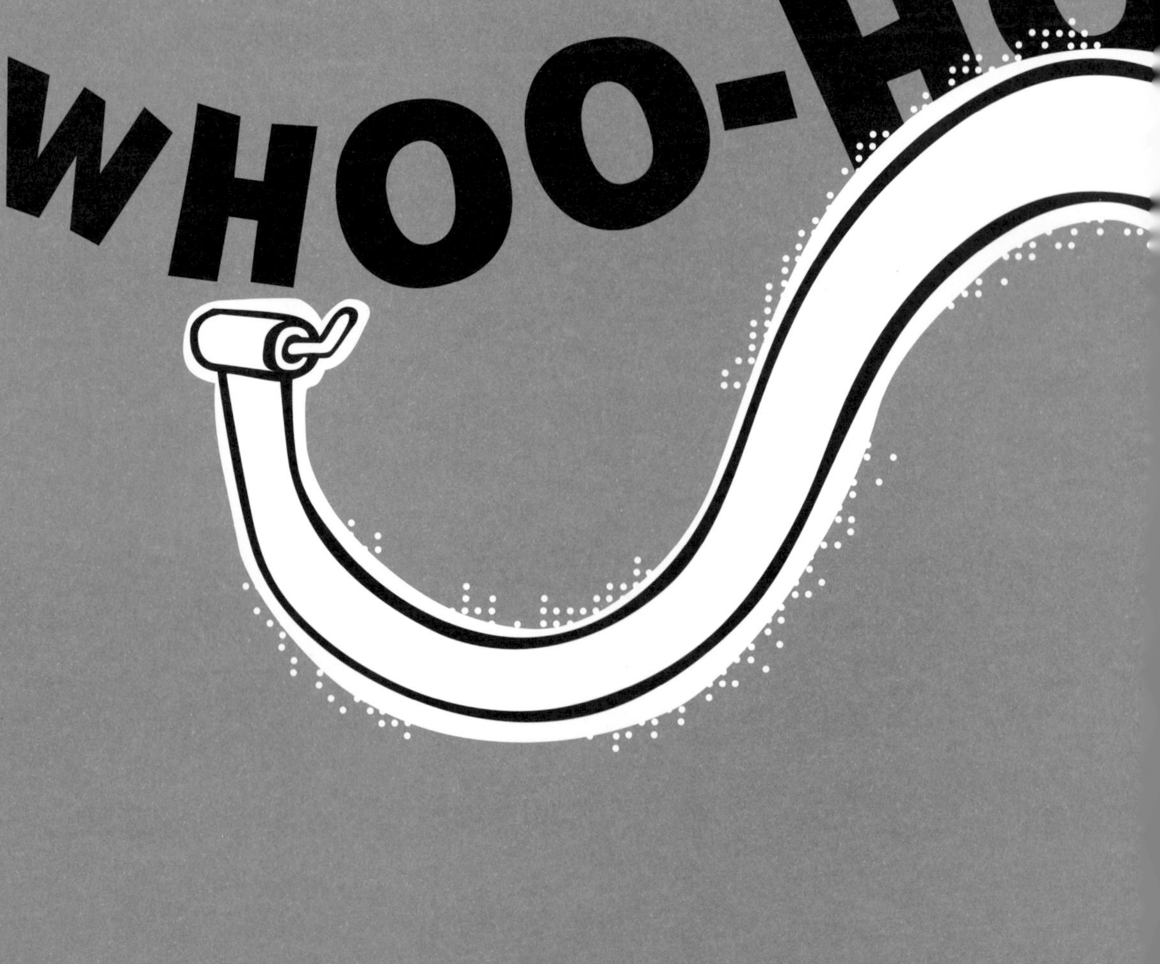
WHOO-HO

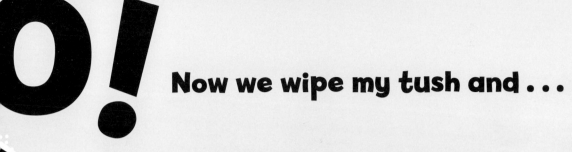

O! Now we wipe my tush and . . .

Bye-bye pee!

Bye-bye poop!

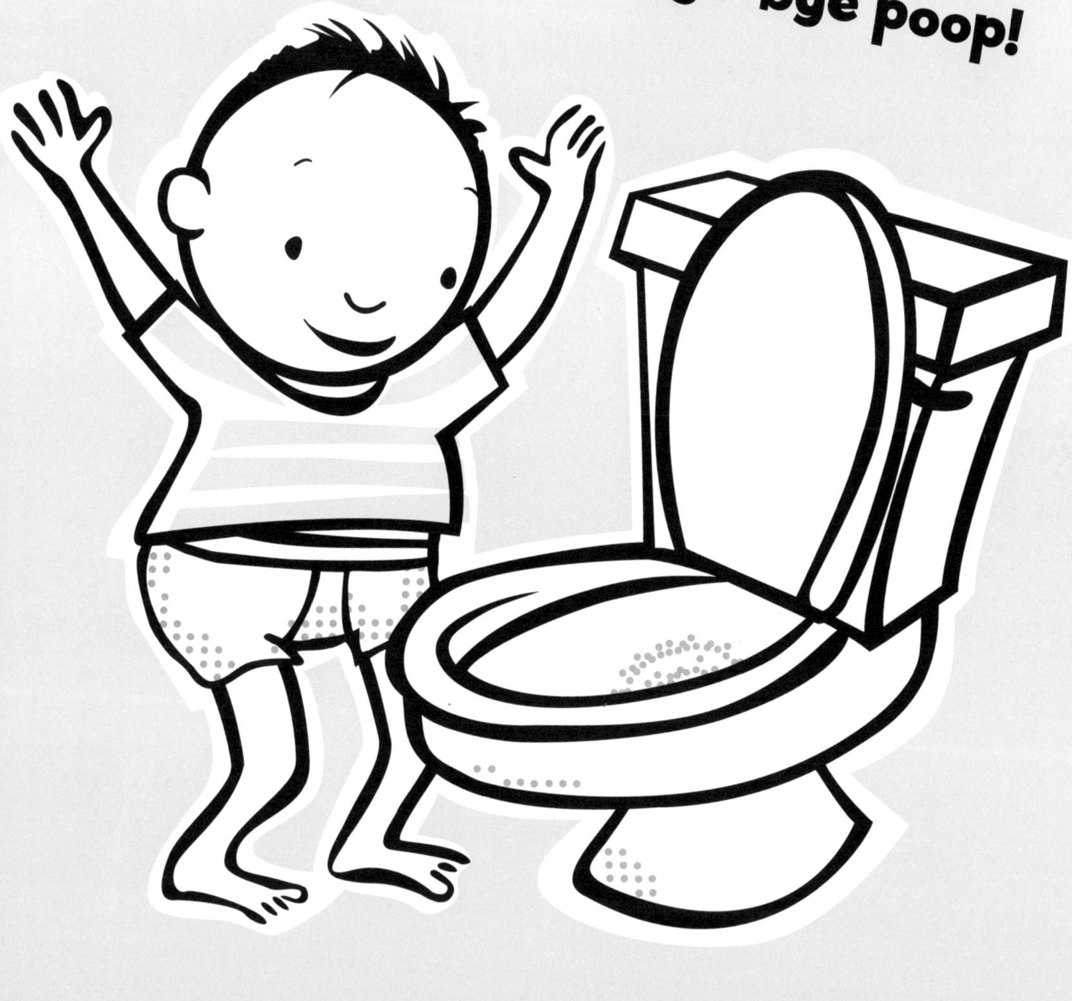

I'M A BIG KID!

I was inspired to write this book by my own experiences potty training my son. Max has taught me that making things fun gets kids on board with just about anything and helps keeps parents sane. He thought it was hilarious when I talked about how babies pee and poop in diapers (the more details and sound effects, the better). He felt encouraged to try when I told him that big kids use the potty. And he felt empowered when I pronounced him a BIG KID: "You did it!"

My pediatrician once told me that no child goes off to college in diapers. For a spell I was convinced my kid would be an exception, but eventually every child wants to be a BIG KID and to conquer challenges.

That's what BIG KID POWER is all about.